For dear wee
Nathan on his very
first birthday.

Much love from
Uncle Crossley &
Auntie Sandi
and a big cheesy
bork from
Jake

2002

Pooh to Grow On

A. A. MILNE

Pooh to Grow On

with decorations by Ernest H. Shepard

Dutton Books · New York

❧ Contents ❧

⇒· Cradle Song ·⇐

O Timothy Tim
  Has ten pink toes,
  And ten pink toes
Has Timothy Tim.
They go with him
  Wherever he goes,
  And wherever he goes
They go with him.

O Timothy Tim
  Has two blue eyes,
  And two blue eyes
Has Timothy Tim.
They cry with him
  Whenever he cries,
  And whenever he cries,
They cry with him.

O Timothy Tim
  Has one red head,
  And one red head
Has Timothy Tim.
It sleeps with him
  In Timothy's bed.
  Sleep well, red head
Of Timothy Tim.

—Now We Are Six

7

❧ Rice Pudding ❧

What is the matter with Mary Jane?
She's crying with all her might and main,
And she won't eat her dinner—rice pudding
     again—
What *is* the matter with Mary Jane?

What is the matter with Mary Jane?
I've promised her dolls and a daisy-chain,
And a book about animals—all in vain—
What *is* the matter with Mary Jane?

What is the matter with Mary Jane?
She's perfectly well, and she hasn't a pain;
But, look at her, now she's beginning again!—
What *is* the matter with Mary Jane?

What is the matter with Mary Jane?
I've promised her sweets and a ride in the train,
And I've begged her to stop for a bit and explain—
What *is* the matter with Mary Jane?

What is the matter with Mary Jane?
She's perfectly well and she hasn't a pain,
And it's lovely rice pudding for dinner again!—
What *is* the matter with Mary Jane?

—*When We Were Very Young*

11

≽· Nursery Chairs ·≼

One of the chairs is South America,
One of the chairs is a ship at sea,
One is a cage for a great big lion,
And one is a chair for Me.

THE FIRST CHAIR

When I go up the Amazon,
I stop at night and fire a gun
    To call my faithful band.
And Indians in twos and threes,
Come silently between the trees,
    And wait for me to land.
And if I do not want to play
With any Indians today,
    I simply wave my hand.
And then they turn and go away—
    They always understand.

THE SECOND CHAIR

I'm a great big lion in my cage,
 And I often frighten Nanny with a roar.
  Then I hold her very tight, and
  Tell her not to be so frightened—
And she doesn't be so frightened any more.

THE THIRD CHAIR

When I am in my ship, I see
   The other ships go sailing by.
A sailor leans and calls to me
   As his ship goes sailing by.
Across the sea he leans to me,
   Above the winds I hear him cry:
"Is this the way to Round-the-World?"
   He calls as he goes by.

THE FOURTH CHAIR

Whenever I sit in a high chair
   For breakfast or dinner or tea,
I try to pretend that it's *my* chair,
   And that I am a baby of three.

Shall I go off to South America?
   Shall I put out in my ship to sea?
Or get in my cage and be lions and tigers?
   Or—shall I be only Me?

—When We Were Very Young

James James
Morrison Morrison
Weatherby George Dupree
Took great
Care of his Mother,
Though he was only three.
James James
Said to his Mother,
"Mother," he said, said he:
"You must never go down to the
end of the town,
if you don't go down with me."

James James
Morrison's Mother
Put on a golden gown,
James James
Morrison's Mother
Drove to the end of the town.
James James
Morrison's Mother
Said to herself, said she:
"I can get right down to the
end of the town
and be back in time for tea."

King John
Put up a notice,
"LOST or STOLEN or STRAYED!
JAMES JAMES
MORRISON'S MOTHER
SEEMS TO HAVE BEEN MISLAID.
LAST SEEN
WANDERING VAGUELY:
QUITE OF HER OWN ACCORD,
SHE TRIED TO GET DOWN TO THE END
OF THE TOWN—FORTY SHILLINGS
REWARD!"

James James
Morrison Morrison
(Commonly known as Jim)
Told his
Other relations
Not to go blaming *him*.
James James
Said to his Mother,
"Mother," he said, said he:
"You must *never* go down to the end of the town
    without consulting me."

James James
Morrison's mother
Hasn't been heard of since.
King John
Said he was sorry,
So did the Queen and Prince.
King John
(Somebody told me)
Said to a man he knew:
"If people go down to the
      end of the town, well,
    what can *anyone* do?"

(Now then, very softly)

J. J.
M. M.
W. G. Du P.
Took great
C/o his M*****
Though he was only 3.
J. J.
Said to his M*****
"M*****," he said, said he:
"You-must-never-go-down-to-the-
      end-of-the-town-
      if-you-don't-go-down-with ME!"

—*When We Were Very Young*

⇒· Halfway Down ·⇐

Halfway down the stairs
Is a stair
Where I sit.
There isn't any
Other stair
Quite like
It.
I'm not at the bottom,
I'm not at the top;
So this is the stair
Where
I always
Stop.

Halfway up the stairs
Isn't up,
And isn't down.
It isn't in the nursery,
It isn't in the town.
And all sorts of funny
    thoughts
Run round my head:
"It isn't really
Anywhere!
It's somewhere else
Instead!"

—*When We Were Very Young*

Teddy Bear

(abridged)

A bear, however hard he tries,
Grows tubby without exercise.
Our Teddy Bear is short and fat
Which is not to be wondered at;
He gets what exercise he can
By falling off the ottoman,
But generally seems to lack
The energy to clamber back.

A bear, however hard he tries,
Grows tubby without exercise.
Our Teddy Bear is short and fat,
Which is not to be wondered at.
But do you think it worries him
To know that he is far from slim?
No, just the other way about—
He's *proud* of being short and stout.

—*When We Were Very Young*

Whenever I walk in a London street,
I'm ever so careful to watch my feet;
    And I keep in the squares,
    And the masses of bears,
Who wait at the corners all ready to eat
The sillies who tread on the lines of the street,
    Go back to their lairs,
    And I say to them, "Bears,
    Just look how I'm walking in all of the squares!"

And the little bears growl to each other,
	"He's mine,
As soon as he's silly and steps on a line."
And some of the bigger bears try to pretend
That they came round the corner to look
	for a friend;
And they try to pretend that nobody cares
Whether you walk on the lines or squares.
But only the sillies believe their talk;
It's ever so portant how you walk.
And it's ever so jolly to call out, "Bears,
Just watch me walking in all the squares!"

—*When We Were Very Young*

✑· Growing Up ·✑

I've got shoes with grown up laces,
I've got knickers and a pair of braces,
I'm all ready to run some races.
  Who's coming out with me?

I've got a nice new pair of braces,
I've got shoes with new brown laces,
I know wonderful paddly places.
  Who's coming out with me?

Every morning my new grace is,
"Thank you, God, for my nice braces:
I can tie my new brown laces."
  Who's coming out with me?

—*When We Were Very Young*

⇒· The Christening ·⇐

What shall I call
    My dear little dormouse?
His eyes are small,
    But his tail is e-nor-mouse.

I sometimes call him Terrible John,
'Cos his tail goes on—
And on—
And on.
And I sometimes call him Terrible Jack,
'Cos his tail goes on to the end of his back.
And I sometimes call him Terrible James,
'Cos he says he likes me calling him names. . . .
    But I think I shall call him Jim,
    'Cos I *am* so fond of him.

—When We Were Very Young

⋙ Knight-in-Armour ⋘

Whenever I'm a shining Knight,
I buckle on my armour tight;
And then I look about for things,
Like Rushings-Out, and Rescuings,
And Savings from the Dragon's Lair,
And fighting all the Dragons there.
And sometimes when our fights begin,
I think I'll let the Dragons win . . .
And then I think perhaps I won't,
Because they're Dragons, and I don't.

—Now We Are Six

✺· The Good Little Girl ·✵

It's funny how often they say to me, "Jane?
    "Have you been a *good* girl?"
    "Have you been a *good* girl?"
And when they have said it, they say it again,
    "Have you been a *good* girl?"
    "Have you been a *good* girl?"

I go to a party, I go out to tea,
I go to an aunt for a week at the sea,
I come back from school or from playing a game;
Wherever I come from, it's always the same:
    "Well?
    "Have you been a *good* girl, Jane?"

It's always the end of the loveliest day:
    "Have you been a *good* girl?"
    "Have you been a *good* girl?"
I went to the Zoo, and they waited to say:
    "Have you been a *good* girl?"
    "Have you been a *good* girl?"

Well, what did they think that I went there to do?
And why should I want to be bad at the Zoo?
And should I be likely to say if I had?
So that's why it's funny of Mummy and Dad,
This asking and asking, in case I was bad,
    "Well?
    "Have you been a *good* girl, Jane?"

           —Now We Are Six

❧ Binker ❧

Binker—what I call him—is a secret of my own,
And Binker is the reason why I never feel alone.
Playing in the nursery, sitting on the stair,
Whatever I am busy at, Binker will be there.

Oh, Daddy is clever, he's a clever sort of man,
And Mummy is the best since the world began,
And Nanny is Nanny, and I call her Nan—
But they can't
See
Binker.

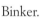

Binker's always talking, 'cos I'm teaching him
        to speak:
He sometimes likes to do it in a funny sort
        of squeak,
And he sometimes likes to do it in a hoodling sort
        of roar . . .
And I have to do it for him 'cos his throat is
        rather sore.

   Oh, Daddy is clever, he's a clever sort of man,
   And Mummy knows all that anybody can,
   And Nanny is Nanny, and I call her Nan—
        But they don't
        Know
        Binker.

Binker's brave as lions when we're running in
      the park;
Binker's brave as tigers when we're lying in
      the dark;
Binker's brave as elephants. He never, never
      cries . . .
Except (like other people) when the soap gets in
      his eyes.

  Oh, Daddy is Daddy, he's a Daddy sort of
      man,
  And Mummy is as Mummy as anybody can,
  And Nanny is Nanny, and I call her Nan . . .
            But they're not
            Like
            Binker.

Binker isn't greedy, but he does like things to eat,
So I have to say to people when they're giving
        me a sweet,
"Oh, Binker wants a chocolate, so could you give
        me two?"
And then I eat it for him, 'cos his teeth are rather
        new.

Well, I'm very fond of Daddy, but he hasn't time
        to play,
And I'm very fond of Mummy, but she sometimes
        goes away,
And I'm often cross with Nanny when she wants
        to brush my hair . . .
But Binker's always Binker, and is certain to
        be there.

—Now We Are Six

⋙· The Engineer ·⋘

Let it rain!
Who cares?
I've a train
Upstairs,
With a brake
Which I make
From a string
Sort of thing,
Which works
In jerks,
'Cos it drops
In the spring,

Which stops
With the string,
And the wheels
All stick
So quick
That it feels
Like a thing
That you make
With a brake,
Not string. . . .

So that's what I make,
When the day's all wet.
It's a good sort of brake
But it hasn't worked yet.

—*Now We Are Six*

Swing Song

Here I go up in my swing
    Ever so high.
I am the King of the fields, and the King
    Of the town.
I am the King of the earth, and the King
    Of the sky.
Here I go up in my swing . . .
    Now I go down.

—Now We Are Six

⇒ Buttercup Days ⇐

Where is Anne?
   Head above the buttercups,
Walking by the stream,
   Down among the buttercups.
Where is Anne?
Walking with her man,
Lost in a dream,
   Lost among the buttercups.

What has she got in that little brown head?
Wonderful thoughts which can never be said.
What has she got in that firm little fist of hers?
Somebody's thumb, and it feels like Christopher's.

Where is Anne?
Close to her man.
Brown head, gold head,
   In and out the buttercups.

—Now We Are Six

≽· Twice Times ·≼

There were Two little Bears who lived in a Wood,
And one of them was Bad and the other was Good.
Good Bear learnt his Twice Times One—
But Bad Bear left all his buttons undone.

They lived in a Tree when the weather was hot,
And one of them was Good, and the other was Not.
Good Bear learnt his Twice Times Two—
But Bad Bear's thingummies were worn right
        through.

They lived in a Cave when the weather was cold,
And they Did, and they Didn't Do, what they were
        told.
Good Bear learnt his Twice Times Three—
But Bad Bear *never* had his hand-ker-chee.

They lived in the Wood with a Kind Old Aunt,
And one said *"Yes'm,"* and the other said
    "Shan't!"
Good Bear learnt his Twice Times Four—
But Bad Bear's knicketies were terrible tore.

And then quite suddenly (just like Us)
One got Better and the other got Wuss.
Good Bear muddled his Twice Times Three—
But Bad Bear coughed *in his hand-ker-chee!*

Good Bear muddled his Twice Times Two—
But Bad Bear's thingummies looked like new.
Good Bear muddled his Twice Times One—
But Bad Bear *never* left his buttons undone.

There may be a Moral, though some say not;
I think there's a moral, though I don't know what.
But if one gets better, as the other gets wuss,
These Two Little Bears are just like Us.
For Christopher remembers up to Twice Times
        Ten . . .
But I keep forgetting where I've put my pen.*

*So I have had to write this one in pencil.

—Now We Are Six

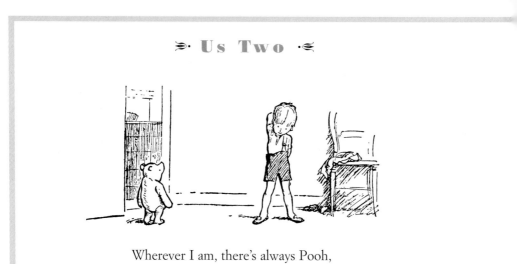

Wherever I am, there's always Pooh,
There's always Pooh and Me.
Whatever I do, he wants to do,
"Where are you going today?" says Pooh:
"Well, that's very odd 'cos I was too.
Let's go together," says Pooh, says he.
"Let's go together," says Pooh.

"What's twice eleven?" I said to Pooh.
("Twice what?" said Pooh to Me.)
"I *think* it ought to be twenty-two."
"Just what I think myself," said Pooh.
"It wasn't an easy sum to do,
But that's what it is," said Pooh, said he.
"That's what it is," said Pooh.

"Let's look for dragons," I said to Pooh.
"Yes, let's," said Pooh to Me.
We crossed the river and found a few—
"Yes, those are dragons all right," said Pooh.
"As soon as I saw their beaks I knew.
That's what they are," said Pooh, said he.
"That's what they are," said Pooh.

"Let's frighten the dragons," I said to Pooh.
"That's right," said Pooh to Me.
"*I'm* not afraid," I said to Pooh,
And I held his paw and I shouted "Shoo!
Silly old dragons!"—and off they flew.
"I wasn't afraid," said Pooh, said he,
"I'm *never* afraid with you."

So wherever I am, there's always Pooh,
There's always Pooh and Me.
"What would I do?" I said to Pooh,
"If it wasn't for you," and Pooh said: "True,
It isn't much fun for One, but Two
Can stick together," says Pooh, says he.
"That's how it is," says Pooh.

—*Now We Are Six*

⋙· The Friend ·⋘

There are lots and lots of people who are always
    asking things,
Like Dates and Pounds-and-ounces and the names
    of funny Kings,
And the answer's either Sixpence or A Hundred
    Inches Long,
And I know they'll think me silly if I get the
    answer wrong.

So Pooh and I go whispering, and Pooh looks
    very bright,
And says, "Well, *I* say sixpence, but I don't suppose
    I'm right."
And then it doesn't matter what the answer ought
    to be,
'Cos if he's right, I'm Right, and if he's wrong,
    it isn't Me.

—Now We Are Six

➣ · The End · ➣

When I was One,
I had just begun.

When I was Two,
I was nearly new.

When I was Three,
I was hardly Me.

When I was Four,
I was not much more.

When I was Five,
I was just alive.

But now I am Six, I'm as clever as clever.
So I think I'll be six now for ever and ever.

—Now We Are Six